Independent order of Odd Fellows

Memorial Addresses Delivered

1882 - upon the deaths of James L. Ridgely, Wm. T. Curry, Taliaferro P.

Shaffner

Independent order of Odd Fellows

Memorial Addresses Delivered
1882 - upon the deaths of James L. Ridgely, Wm. T. Curry, Taliaferro P. Shaffner

ISBN/EAN: 9783337402334

Printed in Europe, USA, Canada, Australia, Japan

Cover: Foto ©Andreas Hilbeck / pixelio.de

More available books at **www.hansebooks.com**

Memorial Addresses

Delivered at

Winchester, October 25, 1882,

Before the

Grand Lodge of Ky., I.O.O.F.

Upon the Deaths of

James L. Ridgely,   Wm. T. Curry,

Taliaferro P. Shaffner,

Together with the

Resolutions adopted by the Grand Lodge and the
Reports of the Committee on Demises.

———

LOUISVILLE.
ROGERS & TULEY, PRINTERS AND STATIONERS.
1882.

*AN ADDRESS UPON THE LIFE AND CHARACTER OF JAMES L. RIDGELY,
DELIVERED AT WINCHESTER, KY., OCTOBER 25, 1882, DURING
THE SESSION OF THE GRAND LODGE OF KENTUCKY,
BY PAST GRAND SIRE M. J. DURHAM.*

IN MEMORIAM.

JAMES LOTT RIDGELY,

Grand Secretary Sovereign Grand Lodge, I. O. O. F.

DIED NOVEMBER 16, 1881.

LADIES, GENTLEMEN, AND BROTHERS:—A great man among Odd
Fellows has fallen. In respect to his memory memorial services,
resolutions of condolence, eulogies upon his life and character have
been had in cities and towns, in the valleys and on the mountain
tops, and from the Atlantic to the Pacific lodge rooms have been
draped with the emblems of mourning, and throughout the wide
domain of Odd Fellowship there has been universal grief and sorrow
over the death of James L. Ridgely. While other grand bodies
have placed on record their estimate of him, it is befitting that we
should say something of his life, labors, and character. To me has
been assigned that duty.

There is in every human bosom a resistless instinct, a constant
longing to testify in some manner its yearning for the loved and the
lost. The fading wreath which affection's hand has entwined about
the tomb of humble poverty, and the mausoleum, with its chiseled

columns—and all the pomp with which grandeur mourns over departed pride, alike remind us of this mournful duty to the dead. Among all civilized people in all times past it has been a beautiful custom to mingle with laments for the dead eulogies upon their well-spent lives. The Greek elegy, the resounding prose of the Roman orator, the beautiful and incisive phrase of the French Academy, and the lofty, poetic verse of Milton and Tennyson have been alike in the one great purpose of teaching the lesson that the highest life is that which is lived for others. The public servant has his reward—that as the tendency of his labors and toils is to take him away from himself and set before him the public good as his highest aim, so the popular heart is willing to overlook his faults and errors and remember only that he was one who has striven to serve his fellow man. It is a charitable sentiment that no one should speak ill of the dead, that their errors, faults, and frailties, whatever they may have been, should be covered by the mantle of oblivion; but it does not follow that their virtues, their noble deeds and valuable services to mankind should remain unrecorded; these should be perpetuated so that their light, which once shone and illumined the pathway of thousands, should not go out in eternal darkness. It is the duty of the living to perpetuate the memory of the great and good, those who have filled high positions with credit to themselves and their country, and who, by their talents, genius, and labor have rendered valuable services to mankind. What is a country without a biography of its distinguished men and its public benefactions? What a blank would be the history of ancient empires and kingdoms if there had been no special mention of their philosophers, poets, heroes, orators, and statesmen. It would have been a shadow without substance, a skeleton divested of its vital, essential parts—life and beauty.

The character of a nation and the criterion of its civilization may be judged by the intelligence, honesty, and purity of those who are appointed its rulers. It is our boast to rejoice in the eminent qualities of the founders of our Republic and those who gave it form and direction in its infancy. While the spirit of freedom pervades the minds of the American people they can not cease to venerate the champions of our independence. The names of Washington, Adams, Franklin, Hamilton, Jefferson, Jay, and Marshall will be handed down from generation to generation, and mentioned with praise as long as free institutions exist on the earth. Those names will be transmitted to posterity as synonymns of great ideas—liberty and self-government. As in nations, so it is with those great institutions which have been organized to ameliorate the condition of mankind; they are judged to a great extent by those who lay deep and broad their foundations and are prominent in their up-building and management, and when these die, their deeds, their characters, their good words and works should be handed down to posterity in letters of living light. Whenever the living cease to remember their dead—a death greater than the mere decay of the human body will sooner or later erase such a people from the map of the world. History, with its great iron pen, will in few words detail their rise, fall, and decay. No one ever dies all forgotten, and no one ever wholly perishes from the face of the earth. The influences of a life even in this world are eternal. The tomb can not enclose them; they escape from its portals and continue to pervade the daily walks of men, like unseen spirits guiding and controlling human thought and action. Who is free from their touch? Whose life and destiny have not been colored, formed, and fashioned by the influences of those who have passed away? The greatest actors on the broad stage of human affairs have pointed back from the loftiest points of their elevation to the mother with her prayers, to the father with his toil and devotion, to unselfish kindred, self-sacrificing friends, and bowed with reverence before the living power associated forever with their names and memories. Every mind and heart reproduces some of its achievements and many of its qualities in the minds and hearts of others after it has gone to far off spheres and realms.　And this is the average of human influence—the silent but mighty stream of causes—producing effect on which mankind from its birth has been borne gradually and steadily forward in its vast career of progress and development.　Now and then, however, the current of this stream receives a new and startling velocity.　Some intellectual force towering over all others of its period occasionally imparts to all the world at once an impetus which condenses the ordinary advancements of years into the thrilling compass of a day.　Then not only individuals, but nations, institutions, and generations become the subjects of an irresistable and everlasting influence; a new era is then noted on the pages of the historian, and new gateways are opened for the onward movements of human amelioration. Such an event occurred in Odd Fellowship in the life and labors of James L. Ridgely.

He was born in the city of Baltimore, January 27, 1807.　He received a liberal education and graduated with honor at Mount St. Mary's College at Emmetsburg.　He studied law and practiced his profession in Baltimore with success—having the confidence of the bench and bar—and discharged ably and faithfully all his duties to his clients.　He was initiated as a member of Columbia Lodge No. 3 on the 27th day of May, 1829, and in the next year he appeared as a Past Grand in the Grand Lodge of Maryland.　He at once took a high position in that lodge.　In 1831 he took his seat in the Grand Lodge of the United States as a representative from the jurisdiction of Maryland.　In 1833 he was elected Grand Master of the Grand Lodge of that State.　In this position he was faithful and efficient, and did much to increase the membership during his term.　In the Grand Lodge of the United States he was placed on some of the most important committees, among them was that which was charged with the duty of revising the ritual, charges, and lectures of the Order.　His fine literary attainments, his great love for our Institution, and his thorough knowledge of the grand principles upon which it rests eminently qualified him for this difficult task.   He was the author of the Past Grand's charge—a composition not excelled in the English language—a production which will be read and re-read, loved, used, and admired as long as Odd Fellowship may exist.   In 1836 he was elected Grand Sire, but he refused :o accept that exalted position.   In 1840 he was elected Grand Secretary of the Grand Lodge of the United States, to fill out the remainder of a term, and in the same year he was again elected Grand Sire, but declined to accept.   No instance like this can be found in the history of the Order.   One competent to fill this high position, a place coveted, sought after, and desired by his most eminent associates, yet he declines because he can do more to up-build, improve, and beautify this Institution in an humbler sphere.   His love of the principles of the Order, his de-desire to reform its workings, to make it a living, grand, powerful Institution out-weighed his ambition for place and power.   In 1841 he was re-elected Grand Secretary, and was successively elected to the same office until in 1881, when he died.

It was in this office he exhibited his wonderful executive ability and his great powers as a writer; it was here he brought order out of chaos; it was here he wrought out those reforms so necessary to the very existence of this Institution.   Although holding this subordinate position he was really the head—the grand motive power which moved the whole Order.   Grand Sires sought and accepted his counsel and advice; and should new questions arise or doubt exist as to the old ones his decision was accepted as the true interpretation of the same.   By the force of his great abilities and his courteous demeanor he won the confidence and admiration of the membership everywhere.   He was a fine speaker, yet sometimes so poetic were his tastes that his speeches were somewhat weakened by a disposition to clothe the coldest logic in flowing, if not in measured terms.   His mastery of language being great, his ready tongue was apt to pander to his tuneful ear and pour out mellow sentences as pleasing in sound as they were sound in logic. His gestures, too, were graceful and in perfect harmony with the euphony of his tones.   He was remarkable for the simplicity of his nature as for the breadth of his mind and for the acumen of his intellect.   Those who analyze the nature and charm of simplicity in a great mind surprise themselves to find the secret of both in the fact that simplicity allied with greatness works its marvel with a sweet unconciousness of its own superior excellence, and it works them out with this unconciousness because it is greater than it knows.   "Talent does what it can; genius does what it must," and in this respect there is a great analogy between the highest goodness and the highest genius, for under the influence of either the spirit of man may scatter light and splendor around it without admiring itself or seeking the admiration of others.   And it was in this sense that the simplicity of Ridgely's nature expressed itself in acts of goodness—and acts of high intelligence—with a spontaniety which hid from himself the transcendent virtue and dignity of the work he was doing, and hence all of his work was done without the slightest taint of vanity or tarnish of self-complacency.   A sense of rectitude presided over all his thoughts and acts.   He had so trained his mind to right thinking, and his will to right feeling and right doing, that this absolute rectitude became a part of his intellectual as well as his moral nature.   He sat at the feet of Nature with as much of candor as of humility, never imparting into his ob. servations the pride of opinion, and never yielding to the seductions of an overweening fancy.   He was sober and discreet in his judgments.   He made no hasty generalization on any subject.   His mind seemed to turn on the "poles of truth."   The *truth* was his guiding star in all his investigations.   He sought it by the plainest methods that earnest inquiry and thorough research could discover. His sources of learning supplied him with rich stores of classical illustrations which were used to both embellish and to intensify his logic.   Deeply impressed with the truth of his own convictions he supported them with an earnestness born of sincerity, with a fullness of information due to his habit of industry and with a power that sprung from large natural ability disciplined by severe training; but he supported them only in a fair and manly way. The solid logic of his arguments, couched in beautiful language and in his array of facts, were intensified in their effect by the clearness of his statement and the strength of his presentation.

Pausing here a moment at this stage in the analysis of Brother Ridgely's mental and moral traits I can not omit to say something of the effect produced on the observer by the happy combination under which these traits were so grouped and confederated in his person as to be mutual compliments to each other. He was courtly in his manners, but a courtliness which sprang from courtesy of heart, and had no taint of affectation or artificiality; he was fastidious in his literary tastes, but he had none of that dilettanteism which is "firmly defective and delicately weak;" he was imbued with simplicity of heart which left him absolutely without guile, yet he was shrewd to protect himself against the arts of the designing; he was severe in his sense of honor, without being sensorious; benevolent, yet inflexibly just; quick in his opinions, yet calm in judgment and patient in labor; tenacious of right, without being controversial; benignant of his moral opinions, yet never sullying the truth; endowed with a strong imagination, yet always making it the handmaid of reason; a prince among men, yet without the slightest alloy of arrogance in the fine gold of his improved intellect; in a word, "good in all his greatness, he was at the same time great in all his goodness." Among all those bright names that have been and are now identified with this Order none shines more brilliantly on the pages of its history than does his; no one has accomplished as much in working out the ends of benevolence and human amelioration, as exemplified and illustrated in the principles of American Odd Fellowship, as our lamented brother. 'Tis true that Wildey, Welch, Mathiot, Marley, and others laid broad and deep the foundation of this temple of benevolence and human benefaction, but it remained for Ridgely to rear the super-structure and ornate and beautify it with architectural grace and loveliness. And what were the results of his labors?

When he entered the Grand Lodge of the United States in 1831 it numbered only eleven jurisdictions, sixty-nine subordinate lodges, and forty-four hundred and fifty members. He lived to see it embrace fifty-nine Grand Lodges, thirty-nine Grand Encampments, seven thousand and forty-eight subordinate lodges, eighteen hundred and twenty-one subordinate encampments, with more than a half million of members, and a revenue received by these lodges of over four million of dollars! What a grand and sublime spectacle this must have been to him! He lived to see it the great moral and social prodigy of the nineteeth century, with no parallel for its growth and development. Its influence had swept across the Atlantic seaboard, and lingering through the vastness of the older States, trembling on the bosom of the great lakes and along our magnificent rivers, swelled in majestic grandeur across the hesperian plains, and calling out from snowy peak to the vernal occident blended at last with the roar of the surf which beats forever on the shores of the great Pacific!

I knew him well and intimately. I have seen him under almost all circumstances—in his office, in the Grand Lodge room, in the family circle; he had the same powers of magnetism everywhere. Wherever the Grand Lodge met, in California, in Atlanta, Philadelphia, Chicago, Ridgely was the magnet around which the whole brotherhood centered. He was the most universally popular man I ever knew. Loving in his nature, his heart yearned to love. His heart was as soft and gentle as a woman's, yet his was a manly nature. Clear in his conceptions, he was steadfast in his opinions. He despised a hypocrite and hated a sham. Brave and manly, yet a cry of distress brought tears to his eyes; stern and decisive in his opinions, yet a friend's distress melted him and a woman's wail commanded him. His life was characterized by purity, simplicity, and benevolence—a purity without a spot, a simplicity which was transparency itself, a benevolence as wide as the spread of our Order and limitless as human want. You who knew him and knew him well can bear cheerful witness to my words. He was as simple as a child—without dissimulation, without guile. He was not smart as some men count smartness—neither have been many of the great spirits of the times. His mind was the crystal depths of a great, pure lake, not the noisy course of a shallow, frothy river. He was a pure man. Pure he was laid to rest without a spot. The product of nearly four score years in this rough world, we lift up his character to-day and say, behold it! the freshness of purity, the stainlessness of childhood are yet upon it. "Grand, is it not, consoling, is it not, that God now and then builds up a man among us of whom we can say, look upon him, walk round about him—you will find no ugly scar, you will find no deformity in him? Grand is it not, consoling, is it not, that now and then in this world of smirched reputations and diseased lives God gives us a whole man—a man whom without a blush we can lift up to the great Master saying, take him again, he is unharmed, he is worthy of Thee?" Methinks even as human hands after his funeral selected from all the floral offerings some few choice ones which they may embalm and preserve so will angel hands, after that the earth has paid its last honors to him, culling over all the offerings which have been laid upon his tomb, select this simple token and hang it high upon heaven's wall—James L. Ridgely, *The Philanthropist.* The influence of this man has taken to itself the wings of the morning and visited the uttermost parts of the earth. It dwells wherever Odd Fellowship exists, shapes and controls its future destiny. Brother Ridgely in one sense is dead; his body, after the labors of a long life, has laid down to rest and to sleep until the great Master shall awaken it again. But even in this world his life has but just begun. As his pure soul enters upon its new career in the regions of immortality, so does the influence which he left behind him here move forward each day to new developments of glory and power in our Order.

We are here to-day performing these duties because he lives in his works and because his undying example still sways and governs our conduct. A half million of brothers bow reverently at his tomb, and thousands upon thousands of widows and orphans are his mourners because of his great labor of love in their behalf. Memorial services can not reach him; he is beyond the sound of praise or the fragrance of its incense. No, we only perform our duty on this occasion by simply recognizing the great good he has wrought out for mankind, attesting his immortality here on earth. Calmly he sleeps beneath the soil of his native State, within the sound of the great city which gave birth to our beloved Order, and which gave him a home and a grave, and with its half million of eager population ever stand night and day as a vigilant sentinel over the tomb of its honored dead. Embowered in the peaceful shades of his own beautiful resting place, through whose stricken boughs the fierce wintry winds chant their requiem, our brother—the father—the husband—the friend—sleeps that sleep that knows no earthly waking. Wreaths will fade and wither on his tomb, perennial flowers will blossom and decay, time will raze the well-rounded mound where he sleeps, monuments will rust and granite crumble, but his deeds are enduring and his name imperishable. But we shall see him again—yes, in a land that is fairer than day—in the full possession and active exercise of those mental powers which have won the admiration and gratitude of his fellow men shall we see him—see him as along the pathway of an unending progress and amid the ever-rising, ever-thickening glories of the universe he makes his way upward into the infinite goal of Friendship, Love and Truth.

The sublime creation of God, which we have known as James L. Ridgely, is endowed with the power of an endless life.

"Eternal form shall still divide
The eternal soul from all beside,
And we shall know him when we meet."

Remembering his career as a man of great labor, as a man who served this Order with singular ability and faithfulness, who was loved and venerated by every circle, who blessed with his friendship the worthiest and the best, whose life added new glory to the human race, "we shall be most fortunate if ever in the future we see his like again." Sometimes we think when a great leader in his department dies the progress of the institution with which he was connected will be retarded or blotted out of existence. Not so if it is founded in truth and right. Presidents and the leading spirits of our country may die, yet the government lives and moves on in its sure progress to greatness. Bishops, prelates and clergymen may die, yet the church lives to be the light and hope of the world. Ridgely, Shaffner and Curry may pass from our midst, yet others rise up to fill their places—while the principles they taught and practiced will never die. My brothers, I then beseech you to imitate their noble examples, cherish and guard well the principles they have vouchsafed to us. When we, and those who shall come after us, shall have discharged our whole duty to ourselves, to mankind and this Order, and when the voice of the angels shall be heard upon the mighty waters when the last note of time shall hoarsely sound from the tomb of immutable ages, and the requiem of the world swells upward and reverberates through boundless space with all created good shall moral virtue as a child of the skies be separated from the ruins of sin and gathered home to the presence of God, when sculptured monuments shall be no more, when honor's gaudy plume shall wither and decay, when magnificent temples shall crumble to the earth, the successful triumphs of Odd Fellowship shall flourish in immortal youth and shine forever on the burnished altars of heaven!

MEMORIAL ADDRESS DELIVERED BEFORE THE GRAND LODGE OF KENTUCKY, I. O. O. F., AT WINCHESTER, BY PAST GRAND PATRIARCH A. H. RANSOM.

IN MEMORIAM.

WILLIAM T. CURRY,

DIED DECEMBER 21, 1882.

MEMBER OF

MONTGOMERY LODGE No. 18,

SHAFFNER ENCAMPMENT No. 10.

Past Grand Master of the Grand Lodge of Kentucky; Past Grand Patriarch of the Grand Encampment of Kentucky; Past Grand Representative to the Sovereign Grand Lodge of the I. O. O. F.

GRAND MASTER AND BRETHREN OF THE GRAND LODGE:—The duty that has been assigned me of preparing a memorial address on the life and character of our lamented brother, William T. Curry, who died since the last annual communication of this Grand Body, fills my heart with sadness, and yet there is an indescribable pleasure in bearing loving testimony to the worth of one who was so highly esteemed by his brethren, one who proved himself worthy of the purest love and strictest confidence, one to whom I felt

myself bound by the ties of strong friendship, even such as existed
between Jonathan and David.   The fear that perhaps my implicit
confidence in and high regard for him might prompt expressions
which by some would be deemed flattery, and the apprehension
that in seeking to avoid such error I might fail to do even adequate
justice to excellencies which by all were known to have been his,
caused me to wish and to express the hope that among his numer-
ous friends some one might have been chosen who would in more
fitting words than I can utter have paid a tribute to our friend's
memory, but having been called upon by the Grand Lodge and the
Grand Encampment to perform this duty, there is nothing left for
me but to comply.

My acquaintance with Brother Curry dates from my first attendance at this Grand Lodge in 1859, three years after he became a
member, and that acquaintance soon ripened into a friendship
which endured until his death.   For more than twenty years had I
the pleasure of knowing him intimately; and knowing him thus, I
feel sure that no labored epitaph, no prosy memorial, no fulsome
eulogy is needed to impress his worth and virtues upon the minds
of those who were numbered among his acquaintances, and I ap-
prehend that a mere recital of some of the leading incidents in
his life-history will be sufficient to show to every one that in all the
relations of life and elements of manhood, as a friend and neigh-
bor, as a husband and father, as an Odd Fellow, and as a Christian
he was in every particular of conduct without fear and without re-
proach; that in all his relations to and intercourse with his fellowmen he proved himself that noblest work of God—an honest man.
Naturally of warm impulses and generous disposition, his life and
actions were tempered by a conscientious regard for right and for
moral law.   Modest in all his good and benevolent actions, he ever
avoided any thing like a public exhibition of them, and they were
seldom well known except to the recipients and to Him who seeth
all things.   In the great day of account when the question is asked,

"When saw we thee an hungered and fed thee, or when saw we thee athirst and gave thee drink, or when saw we thee naked and clothed thee, or when saw we thee sick and in prison and minis- tered unto thee?" methinks the blessed One will smile more sweetly than is His wont, and that His voice will be kinder and gentler than usual when He shall say to our brother, "Inasmuch as ye did it unto the least of these, my brethren, ye did it unto Me."

Brother William T. Curry was born in the city of Harrodsburg, Ky., January 6, 1823. There he passed his youth; there on ar- riving at the proper age he engaged in business; there he was married; there he lived his entire life; and when his labor on earth was ended there, on the 21st of April, 1882, he died at the age of 59 years, and there in the beautiful cemetery adjoining his native city he was buried. It was in the early spring, when the opening flowers in their eagerness to burst the bonds which held them cap- tive during the long months of winter seemed to indicate the happy release of our brother from his earthly bonds; when the clear and cloudless sky opened as it were to the vision of the bereaved ones the limitless route from time to eternity; when the king of day as he pursues his majestic course through the heavens, causing the heart of man to rejoice at the ushering in of the advent of another seed-time and harvest, reminded them of the advent of our brother into the better world beyond the grave; when the exultant carols of the feathered songsters on the return to their haunts of former years were symbolic of the songs which greeted our brother on his entry into the home of the blessed; when all nature seemed to have put on her richest garniture and to be singing the song of resurrec- tion and immortality, emblematic of the future of our departed brother. It was at this time, when the season and all nature were expressive of our hope that with our brother all was well, that in the presence of a large assemblage of his brethren of the mystic tie from his own and the neighboring lodges, and also of numbers of his friends and neighbors who had assembled to testify their appreciation of the worth of one who had always lived among them and who was known and loved by them, that the last offices which the living can render to the dead were performed by Past Grand Sire Durham in accordance with the ritual of our Order, and our brother's worn out garment, the tenantless body, was laid in the grave— earth to earth, ashes to ashes, dust to dust—there to rest until the great day of resurrection when at the sound of the last trump all shall be assembled before the judgment seat to give account of the deeds done in the body, whether they be good or whether they be evil.   And it seems but fitting that these Grand Bodies should express to his family the high appreciation of his brethren in Odd Fellowship of the manly and useful life of him whom they have lost and we deplore, and that his last eulogy should be pronounced now in this peaceful autumn time when the season seems naturally symbolic of his well-spent career, ripening through nearly three score years until reaped and gathered into the garner of the Grand Master of the universe.

In February, 1842, at the early age of 19, Brother Curry united with the Presbyterian Church, of which during his entire life he was a consistent member, and in which he served as deacon and treasurer for many years.

On July 20, 1847, when 24 years old, he was united in marriage to her who now survives him, and who mourns the loss of him whose love was of her very life a part.   He had five children, four sons and one daughter, all of whom survive him to mourn his loss and revere his memory.   It was in the relation of husband and father that his character shone with its brightest luster.   Through all the various changes of life, whether cheered by the smiles of prosperity or depressed by the clouds of adversity, whether in the full enjoyment of bodily health or suffering from the wasting of sickness and disease, at all times and under all circumstances he was ever the same—faithful, constant, tender, and devoted to the choice of his youth.   His naturally warm heart and generous disposition—disciplined and regulated by the principles and precepts of Odd Fellowship, chastened and strengthened by the practice of those duties to his brethren in distress consequent upon his membership in the lodge, elevated and spiritualized by the religion which he embraced in his youth and which during his whole life was not merely a form and profession, but an active principle and his daily guide, controlling his actions and conduct—united with and assisted by the gentle influences, wise discrimination and loving cooperation of her who was in all respects worthy to be the life-partner of such a man, were well calculated to make his married life what it was beyond question, one of continued and unalloyed happiness, his home the haven of joy and comfort, and his house the mansion of peace and content. Such a home seems almost too sacred to be spoken of in public on any occasion, but I feel that otherwise justice could not be done our brother. Even as I could not comprehend in all its fullness the happiness of that home until I had been a recipient of its cordial and generous hospitality—an occasion highly appreciated at the time and on which memory fondly lingers as one of the most delightful episodes of my own life—it was not strange that they were looked upon as being specially favored by Providence or that their names were considered synonyms of domestic peace and happiness. And it was to be expected that the children of such parents, nurtured and reared under the ennobling and happy influences of such a home, should have the loving characteristics of both their parents, and become, as we find is the case, worthy descendants of so noble a sire, ready and prepared to do their duty in the battle of life, valuable additions to society and worthy recipients of the good name left to them—a rich legacy by one of whom we may well say: "Blessed are the dead who die in the Lord, for they rest from their labors and their works do follow them."

As an Odd Fellow, Brother Curry was one of whom the jurisdiction of Kentucky may well be proud, and whose example we all might follow with credit to ourselves and benefit to the Order. Initiated in Montgomery Lodge No. 18, at Harrodsburg, Ky., but six months after its institution, when he was twenty-two years of age, the teachings of our Order found in him a willing adherent and a hearty supporter. It was not enough for him that his name was simply enrolled as a member, or that he merely paid his dues and left to others the labor and responsibility of performing the work of the lodge. He at once took the degrees, passed through the subordinate offices, and on the first of July, 1847, was installed Noble Grand, and so constant and faithful was his attendance at the lodge that he was absent from his station but once during his official term. Nor did his efforts cease upon receiving the highest honors that could be conferred in the lodge, as is too often the case, but desirous of promoting its interests he accepted the office of Secretary, which responsible position he held for many years. He was for a long time District Deputy Grand Master, and the duties of that office were faithfully performed by him to the satisfaction of all concerned, to the benefit of the lodge and to the prosperity of the Order. In the practical exemplification of the teachings of our Order Brother Curry was pre-eminent. The command of our laws—to visit the sick, relieve the distressed, bury the dead, and educate the orphan found in him a ready response and a cheerful obedience; no labor was too arduous, no call too untimely, no trouble too exactory, and no distance too great to deter him from responding to the calls of duty in that direction. Whenever there was any want to relieve, any sorrow to assuage, any misery to ameliorate, or any tears to dry, there he could be found ready to soothe the anguish of those in trouble, to raise the drooping spirits of the disconsolate, and to pour balm and consolation into the ear of the afflicted. When the attempt was made in this jurisdiction to establish a home for the widows and an institution for the education of the orphans of deceased Odd Fellows he was one of the foremost in advocating its claims, and secured material support for its erection and maintenance, not only from his own means and those of his lodge, but from the citizens in the community where he lived. Whilst fully carrying out the duties enjoined by the Order in these respects he also recognized that in addition to relieving the necessities of our brethren in distress the principles of the Order point to higher duties and aims in life, and in his association with his brethren in the lodge he endeavored by practice as well as by precept to show that fraternity is the corner stone upon which the whole superstructure of Odd Fellowship is based, and that one of the great lessons taught by our ritual is "The fatherhood of God and the brotherhood of man;" while in his intercourse with the world at large he illustrated the great truth ever present in our lessons: "Whatsoever ye would others should do unto you, do ye even so unto them." That his labor and attention in the lodge were promotive of benefit is shown by the interest that was always manifested in its meetings and the ever prompt and constant attention of the members; and that his life and conduct had its influence on those not affiliated with the Order is evident from the interest in its welfare manifested by the whole community, the desire expressed by those eligible to membership to become enlisted under its banner, and the fact that appeals for admission into the lodge were made and granted until nearly all had been received therein. I remember that upon one occasion, when at the lodge in company with the Grand Officers, that a desire was expressed to witness the rendition of the work by Montgomery Lodge, and answer was given that every desirable and available man in the place was already a member of the lodge, but that as some young men living there had expressed their determination to join the lodge on arriving at the required age, if a visitation were made at that time the wish could be gratified.

Not only in his own lodge was our brother's influence felt and appreciated, but all over the jurisdiction were his efforts productive of good to the Order. For many years his business called him to different parts of the state, and wherever he might be—if there was a lodge in that location—there he was to be found encouraging the brethren by his presence, instructing them in the work, counseling as to their duties, obligations, and privileges as members of the lodge, and interesting them by his remarks on the "good of the Order."

His membership in Shaffner Encampment No. 10, at Harrodsburg, was a counterpart of that in the lodge—rapidly passing from the initiatory to the highest rank in the encampment. Ever faithful and constant and always laboring with well-directed zeal for the good of the Order and the welfare of his brethren, the result was that the encampment rose to the front rank and was looked to as a model for others in the jurisdiction; and it was a well-merited token of approval when its generous and noble-hearted namesake, in recognition of the high regard in which the encampment was held by him in common with his brethren, presented a beautiful silver service, which has ever been preserved by them with zealous care and still forms a prominent feature in the ornamentation of their encampment-room.

In July, 1856, he became a member of the Grand Lodge of Kentucky, and the same year he entered the Grand Encampment. In both these bodies he manifested the same zeal and labored with the same earnestness that had characterized him in the subordinate bodies, and the records of those Grand Bodies teem with evidence of his work therein. He was present at every session, with the exception of one year, from the time of his entry until the year 1880, when he was prevented from attending by the sickness which after eighteen months of intense suffering terminated his life.

Of all his colleagues in the Grand Lodge in 1856 but very few are members of the Grand Lodge at this present session. Past Grand Sire Durham, Grand Treasurer Morris, Grand Secretary White, and Grand Guardian Hinkle are nearly all that are left—some having completed their labors on earth have been called to their rest and reward; some have removed to other fields of labor; others have given place to younger and more active members, while others still having become weary of well-doing have ceased working in our labor of love.

In the long list of our illustrious dead, among those who in the many years past have been called from our midst, there are few if any whose names will be cherished by the survivors with more affection, whose kindly and cheerful presence will be more severely missed, whose loss will be more deeply felt, whose labor was more valuable, or whose counsels were more heeded than those of our lamented brother, both in the Grand Lodge and in the Grand Encampment.

In 1859 Bro. Curry was elected Grand Patriarch, and in 1867 he was elected Grand Master, and in both positions the record of his administration shows many evidences of his marked ability and success in promoting the interests of the Order.

In 1869 he was elected by the Grand Encampment of Kentucky a Representative to the Sovereign Grand Lodge, and so well and faithfully did he perform his duty in that station that he was continued as such until 1876, eight consecutive years. His service in that Grand Body of one year on the Committee on Petitions, two years on the Committee on Finance, and five years on the Committee on State of the Order shows that in that body he also extended the same patient labor and earnest zeal in the performance of duty that had characterized him elsewhere and that won for him the high regard in which he was held by his associates.

From subordinate lodge and encampment, from state and Sovereign Grand Lodge, from his brethren of the Order every where—from one and all comes an attesting voice that Past Grand Master, Past Grand Patriarch, Past Grand Representative William T. Curry was ever punctual in his attendance, zealous in the discharge of his duties, punctilious in his obedience to the laws of the Order, and courteous in his intercourse with all his brethren. I need not say more if I would. He leaves behind a record that justifies what one brother says of him, "He was a devoted brother, a loving husband, a kind and affectionate father, a good citizen, an honest man, a faithful Odd Fellow, and a true Christian." Who among us would not be satisfied if the same could be truthfully written on his tomb?

And now friend and brother, farewell; thy grave is flooded with the chastened sunlight of autumn like the evening glory of a well-spent life. Light lie the earth on thy clay, and may thy spirit welcome us all when our day's work is done to the ranks of the brotherhood who have crossed the river into the unseen land. To his family, to his friends, to his brethren, especially those among us who are on the decline of life, whose heads are frosted with the snows of many years and who are becoming conscious of the approach of the time when the grasshopper will be a burden, and the days will come when we shall be weary of them, to us all the departure of our brother is the severing of another link which bound us to earth; but with the eye of faith we can look forward and see that another link has been forged that shall never be severed, our brother in that unknown world beyond the river eagerly watching for the day to come when his outstretched hand will grasp our feeble arm and he shall welcome us to the home of the blessed to enjoy the smiles of our Grand Master for evermore.

MEMORIAL ADDRESS DELIVERED BEFORE THE GRAND LODGE OF KENTUCKY, I. O. O. F., AT WINCHESTER, BY PAST GRAND MASTER GEORGE W. MORRIS.

IN MEMORIAM.

Viae gloriae ne nisi, ad sepulcrum ducunt.

"THE PATHS OF GLORY LEAD BUT TO THE GRAVE."

TALIAFERRO PRESTON SHAFFNER,

BORN IN

FAIRQUAIR COUNTY, VA.,

A. D. 1818,

DIED AT TROY, N. Y.,

December 11, 1881.

MEMBER OF

CHOSEN FRIENDS LODGE No. 2,

MOUNT HOREB ENCAMPMENT No. 1,

Past Grand of the Grand Lodge of Kentucky; Past Grand Patriarch of the Grand Encampment of Kentucky; Grand Representative to the Sovereign Grand Lodge of the I. O. O. F.

Under the mysterious dispensations of an all-wise Providence we as individuals and as an organized body are annually arrested in the course of our benevolent pursuits and required to pause, at least momentarily, and made to realize in grief and sadness the vanity of all worldly things, the instability of wealth and power, the certain decay of all earthly greatness, and the frailness of our hold upon human life Since our last annual meeting a great leader has fallen. A majestic and towering form, which was wont to move among us, and upon which we were accustomed to gaze with feelings of pride, respect, admiration, and affection, has disappeared, and the places which knew him so well know him no more. That ever restless brain, that noble and true heart which throbbed for other's woes, that generous, open hand which knew so well the force and power of friendship's grasp, that sweet, soft, familiar voice attuned to notes of friendship, love, and truth, to which we all loved so well to listen, conveying as it did to our ears those words of encouragement, counsel, and wisdom, coming to us with all the power and pathos of magnetic inspiration—these have all passed away never to return, for he who was the instrument of their force, vitality, and inspiration "sleeps his last sleep, has fought his last battle. No sound shall awake him to glory again."

Nearly half a century ago, on a hot summer morning in the month of July, there might have been seen wending his way up Bullitt street, in the city of Louisville, a tall, slender youth, carrying on his shoulder a small hair trunk, which contained a few articles of coarse wearing apparel, and which embraced all his earthly possessions. He had just landed at the Louisville wharf from St. Louis, Mo., to which place he had come from the interior of that State on foot, and having no money was allowed by the kind captain of the boat, who took pity on him, to travel with him to Louisville as a deck passenger.

His object in coming to Louisville was to find a lady who, he had been informed, resided there, and who was a dear friend of his deceased mother. After reaching Main Street he began his inquiries as to the whereabouts of his "Aunt Mary Eubank," as he styled her, and after wandering about the city for several hours he was finally directed to the humble abode of her who afterward proved to be a friend and a mother to him.

And thus was introduced upon the stage of active life the friendless orphan boy, young Taliaferro Preston Shaffner, who, though born in Virginia, ever claimed Kentucky as his home, and who has left a name which during a third of a century has been as familiar in Odd Fellowship as household words, and an impress in the world of science, literature, and art equalled by few and surpassed by no unofficial American citizen.

Shortly after he came to Louisville he obtained a situation as a clerk in a retail clothing store on what was then known as Wall Street. In this capacity he continued for a few years, when he concluded to take a new departure, and began the study of law. After being admitted to the bar he determined to become conspicuous in his profession and to let his light shine, and to the great astonishment of his legal brethren, who in those days were not given to advertising, the front of his office he covered over with the names of all the states and territories of the Union, he having received the appointment of notary public and commissioner of deeds for them all.

Full of energy, and being of a nervous temperament, he was not satisfied to remain quietly in his office and wait for clients, nor had he the means or influential friends to aid him in his efforts to gratify his laudable ambition to advance rapidly in his profession. He therefore became attracted to the subject of telegraphy, then in its infancy, and soon became absorbed in it, with what results the legal contests in which he was engaged and which he fought step by step through the various courts in defence of the patent rights of Morse will fully attest.

He afterward became associated with Morse in establishing telegraph lines through Kentucky, and the first telegraph pole erected in the state was at the southeast corner of Market and Third Streets, in Louisville, placed there with his own hands.

Between the years 1848 and 1853 he constructed a line from Cincinnati to Frankfort, and from the latter place to Louisville. After this he ran a line from Louisville to Paducah; these completed, he began the construction of one to Nashville by way of Bardstown, and ultimately extended it to New Orleans.

In the year 1853 he made an entended tour through several countries of Europe in the interest of telegraphy and railroads, and after his return to this country he published a work on telegraphy which was accepted as authority on that subject both in Europe and America. In the year 1856 he, with eight other gentlemen, conceived the idea of placing a telegraph cable across the Atlantic ocean, and again visited Europe, this time to perfect arrangements for laying a submarine cable. This was done. The obstacles encountered in the transmission of messages over it caused an effort to be made to select a more advantageous route, and for this purpose a vessel was fitted out and placed at his disposal; in it he made a voyage to Labrador, Greenland, thence to Iceland, Scotland, and Denmark, making deep sea soundings for a route by way of these countries. This survey was entirely satisfactory, but the failure of other projects following that of the first Atlantic cable shook public confidence and caused this route to be abandoned.

In this survey he preserved in bottles the substances brought from the bottom of the ocean in his deepest sea soundings, took them to Hamburg, where they were analyzed by one of the most celebrated chemists of Europe, and in which animal life was discovered. This demonstrated the existence of life at the bottom of the ocean, a fact not previously credited among scientists, and when established necessitated some marked changes in physical geography.

In 1861 he again visited Europe, and while there wrote a history of the United States, published in two quarto volumes, in which he.

gave an elaborate review of the causes which led to the war of secession. This work met with ready and extensive sale from the well-known reputation of its author in Europe and his presumed knowledge of and familiarity with the subjects treated of.

During his sojourn there he became a member of several literary and scientific societies of Great Britain and the continent, and formed the acquaintance of many of the most distinguished men of Europe, among whom he classed Fariday, Huxley, Tyndal, Bismarck, and Gladstone, as his personal friends. He was received and treated with marked courtesy by Queen Victoria, the kings of Denmark, Sweden, and Norway, and the Czar of all the Russias, and honors were conferred on him seldom before vouchsafed to any private American. He was decorated with the orders of the Commander of the Sword, Commander of St. Orlaf, and Commander of the Donnabrog, all of which were marks of great respect and distinction.

During the Austro-Prussian-Danish war of 1862 he tendered his services to the King of Denmark, which were promptly accepted by creating him a colonel of artillery, in which capacity he served with great credit until the close of that war.

In 1864 he returned home and was appointed to a position on the staff of General Grant and served with him until the close of the war. He took part in the capitulation of Gen. Lee at Appomattox, and Gen. Grant declared that his narration of that surrender was the most graphic, complete, and truthful account of it that he had ever seen.

After the war closed he turned his attention again to pursuits which required scientific and chemical knowledge, and in the investigation and pursuit of which his efforts, as formerly, were crowned with signal success.

At the time of his decease he was largely interested in establishments which he had founded for the manufacture of nitro-glycerine and giant powder, the difficulties of which in their application to practical purposes had been overcome by his scientific and thorough knowledge.

We turn now to view him in the light in which he presented himself in an altogether different sphere. However bright that light shone in the outer world it was reserved to the inner temple of Odd Fellowship to call forth and put in vigorous exercise those hidden springs of the heart which like a torch "the more it's shook it shines," the result of which was to develop to a remarkable degree those virtues and characteristics which left behind him in his eventful and rugged pathway a power, an influence, and an effulgence which

> "Through the ages
> Living in historic pages
> Will brighter glow
> And gleam immortal."

According to his own account he began his earnest life-work as a man in this Order. In after years, alluding to it, he said : "As soon as I became a member I saw there was a chance for me to become useful. I appreciated the honor that had been conferred upon me in considering me worthy to become a member, and at once made up my mind that it devolved on me to compensate by reciprocating the honor. I derived so much good by way of instruction during lodge meetings that I shall never be able to fill the measure of my obligations to the Order, except in ever feeling a sense of gratitude to it."

Most faithfully did he redeem this pledge.

As a young and enthusiastic Odd Fellow he labored in season and out of season for its advancement. Possessed with a laudable ambition to excel in whatever he undertook, it was but a few years after he became a member before his name as a speaker and writer was known throughout the jurisdiction of Kentucky. Nor were his brethren tardy in acknowledging his services and worth, for the records of the Order show that he was advanced to positions of responsibility and honor in it more rapidly than any one who had preceded him.

After he became absorbed in the business affairs of life which took him from his home, friends, and country for a long period of time, he, amid all his wanderings, privations, and dangers would turn with anxious and longing eyes to his old Kentucky home with all the affection and devotion of God's chosen people who in their wanderings would daily turn their faces toward their beloved and devoted city and exclaim: "If I forget thee, O Jerusalem, let my right hand forget her cunning; if I do not remember thee, let my tongue.cleave to the roof of my mouth." Referring to his absence he on another occasion remarked: " During my long absence from you how fondly did I revive a recollection of the early scenes of this Order. Oftentimes as I lay on the snow and ice in the far North did I revolve in my mind old associations at home. I was not sure of ever returning, as my exploring life involved me in so many dangers. At all times, however, I thought of home and pined to be with you again. And now after these many years of separation have passed—after roaming over the world, living a checkered life, sometimes in affluence, at other times in poverty and in want; sometimes the guest of sovereigns, princes, potentates, and learned societies, and at other times feasting with the Esquimaux on raw fish, and glad to get it; after one of the most eventful lives that has ever happened to an American of ordinary capacity—I find myself again on the banks of the beautiful Ohio, at home among those I love so well, and with precisely the same zeal and ardent devotion to our Order that I had a third of a century ago."

From and after his return home until his death he was ready to dedicate his time, talents, and energies to the cause of Odd Fellowship in his own lodge and encampment, the Grand Lodge and Encampment, and the Sovereign Grand Lodge of the I. O. O. F. And without going into detail as to what he did accomplish as the result of his increasing efforts, let it suffice to say that no truer, no more devoted Odd Fellow, no one who has ever had the highest interests of this Order more closely entwined around the heart, no one in all its annals since it was first planted on Kentucky soil presents a brighter or more distinguished record than Taliaferro P. Shaffner.

And thus he continued in the good work, regarding Odd Fellowship in its influence upon mankind as the grandest, noblest, and most potent human Institution in the world, worthy of all commendation and entitled to the best efforts of every true lover of his race.

This address, however, would be incomplete did it fail to record in connection with this remarkable life his firm reliance on a higher power. No one familiar with his writings, and especially with his inner life, can fail to have discovered his profound reverence for things sacred and his strong convictions of the truths of Christianity. When a young man, starting out in life, he embraced religion and united with the Methodist Episcopal Church, and for several years thereafter was an active and prominent member of it. In all his subsequent wanderings over the world he never forgot his first love, but adhered strictly to his early convictions. He was not merely a believer in the Bible, but accepted without mental reservation its teachings, including its great doctrine of grace by which alone through faith rested his hope of salvation. To this may, in a great measure at least, be attributed that mildness of manner, that sweetness of temper, that gentleness, broad philanthropy, readiness to forgive injuries, that heart devoid of malice and overflowing with kindness and love to his fellowmen which were the peculiar characteristics of his nature.

About two years ago, when he lay in a most critical condition, vibrating between life and death as it were, the writer took occasion to converse with him touching his views of the life beyond the grave. His mind at the time was bright and clear, and in a beautiful train of thought he unfolded the subject in which he grounded his hope of salvation through a Crucified Redeemer, expressing his free and unqualified belief in the doctrine of a future state, his willingness and readiness to meet death with composure, having made his peace with his Maker. Such was his testimony at that critical moment of his history.

On the night of December 3, 1881, the lodges and encampments of Louisville were convened to give expression of their feelings at the great loss which had overtaken the Order throughout the world in the death of James L. Ridgely. Bro. Shaffner was present, and it seems most fitting that his last public utterance on earth should have been pronounced upon his life-long friend. His exordium on that occasion comes to us from the very portals of the tomb. It was as follows:

"My Brethren—The devotees of Odd Fellowship throughout the world are weeping over the loss of their veteran chieftain, James L. Ridgely, who is no more. From the dawn of manhood to the setting sun of old age his pathway through life was decorated with useful bloom. The beautiful rose that glistened in the sunbeams of the morning has withered upon the stalk and its leaves have drooped and fallen to mother earth.

"All that was mortal of Ridgely now lies in the ever-burning furnace of time. He has not had a peer, and he will never have a successor. He was a remarkable man in every position that he occupied in society, and faithful in the discharge of every duty required of him by civil, fraternal, and religious associations.

"And though from his own choice he held but a subordinate administrative office in the Sovereign Grand Lodge, yet his transcendent abilities accomplished for this Institution the most brilliant success."

Within one brief week after the lamented Shaffner gave utterance to these beautiful and truthful words, yet not until after having attained a plane of eminence in this Order such as few have ever reached, and having witnessed with laudable pride the beneficial results of his life labors, suddenly and without warning, away from his home, the summons came to him, when after a brief and heroic struggle with the "King of Terrors" the silver cord was loosed and the golden bowl was broken.

As the lightning writes in legible characters its fiery pathway across the dark cloud and then disappears, so the race of man walking amid the surrounding shades of mortality glitters for a moment through the gloom and then vanishes from our sight. And so too, my brethren, our labor of love and duty on this earth will soon be ended and we called to join that mighty army who have crossed the river of death.

Soft be the bed of our departed brother and friend, and sweet be the clods of the valley unto him; with fragrance eternal be his memory green in our recollections and affections, and while we that memory most fondly cherish let us one and all his sterling virtues emulate.

Death is the inexorable penalty we must all pay. It is an inflexible and an inherent law, binding upon every thing animate and inanimate. It is written alike upon the giant oak which has withstood the storms of a century, and the sensitive plant which droops and withers at the slightest touch; upon the falling leaf, the beautiful flower, the silent and majestic mountain; upon the brow of helpless infancy, the stalwart frame of vigorous manhood, and the trembling limbs of age. It has no limitation, save the measure of our days which our Creator hath prescribed, and hath ordained that "Dust thou art and unto dust thou shalt return," or in the language of our ritual, "All that is born must die."

"But it can not be that this earth is man's only abiding place. It can not be that our life is but a bubble cast up by the vast ocean of eternity to float for a moment on the wave and then sink into deep darkness and nothingness. Else why this constant longing of the soul after immortality? Why is it that aspirations which leap like angels from the temples of our hearts are forever wandering about unsatisfied? Why is it that yonder stars, which hold their festival around the midnight throne, are set so far above the grasp of our limited faculties forever mocking us with their unapproachable glory? Why is it that the bright forms of human beauty are presented to our view and then taken from us, leaving the thousand streams of our affection to flow back in cold and Alpine torrents upon our hearts?" No, no; it can not be; for not only the page of inspiration, but nature's every page reveals in characters of living light the great truth that it is not all of life to live, that death does not end all, that we are born for a higher, a nobler destiny than that of earth.

Yes, my brethren, these brilliant lights which have adorned and studded the firmament of Odd Fellowship are not put out. They are but hid for the moment behind the gloomy shadow of what we call death only to reappear in immortal beauty, purity, and brilliancy, to shine forever.

> * "There is no death; the stars go down
> To rise upon some fairer shore;
> And bright in heaven's jeweled crown
> They shine forever more."

> "There are some rocks God planted on the shore
> To fix the boundary 'twixt land and sea;
> There are some men who mid the strife and roar
> Are moral light-houses where so 'r they be.

> "They also serve who only stand and wait,
> Yet folded hands would ill become us all;
> The world has need of those who conquer fate,
> And there are men—victorious as they fall.

> "Of all such men thou wast a noble peer;
> Thy life o'er ours shall cast a heedfull spell,
> And now we pay the tribute of a parting tear,
> And say, 'Dear Shaffner, hail, farewell.'"

---

*This gem is usually ascribed to Bulwer. Its author, however, is J. L. McCreary, an American, who at the present time is a clerk in the Department of the Interior at Washington.

REPORTS and RESOLUTIONS

ADOPTED BY THE

Grand Lodge of Ky., I. O. O. F.

Past Grand Master M. J. Durham submitted the following report:

To the Grand Lodge of Kentucky;

The Committee on Demises beg leave to report that during the past year death has invaded our brotherhood, and has taken from our midst some of our most distinguished as well as our most experienced and trusted members. Their deaths are a serious loss to us, but we should imitate their noble examples, and emulate their many striking virtues. Shaffner, Curry, Merrick, Pindell, Dean, Shaller, Grief, and Holland, of our own jurisdiction, after years of devotion to the principles of our Order, have gone to reap their rewards, we hope, in the Grand Lodge on high. We would not be unmindful of the loss we and the Order everywhere has sustained in the death of Brother Ridgely after a long life of usefulness and great activity at his post of duty; he, too, has gone to his long last resting place. We should not indulge in fruitless repinings at the loss of these brothers, but borrowing inspiration and incentive from the sublime example left us in the purity of their lives and the beneficence of the works which still follow them, we should be the more zealous in the upbuilding of the great and grand principles of this Order.

We refer to and make part hereof the accompanying synopsis of the lives and characters of these brothers, the extended addresses in regard to Brothers Ridgely, Shaffner, and Curry, and the resolutions concerning Brother Ridgely.

Fraternally reported,

M. J. DURHAM,   B. F. PULLEN,

G. W. MORRIS,   C. W. HARRIS.

A. H. RANSOM,

Which was adopted by a rising vote.

Past Grand Master Geo. W. Morris, from the same committee, submitted the following report:

To the Grand Lodge of Kentucky:

To cherish the memory and to commemorate the virtues of the loved who have gone before us is the grave duty which devolves upon your committee at each recurring session of the Grand Lodge.

In the language of him of whom we now speak, our venerated and beloved Shaffner, "Every year we are called to lament the departure of a brother on the journey through the dark valley of the shadow of death. Every year we are called to feed the ever-burning furnace of time with one or more of our chosen few."

To speak of the honored and lamented Shaffner and to recount his eminent services to this Order in the subordinate lodges and encampments, the Grand Lodge and Grand Encampment of Kentucky, would be to almost reproduce the history of Odd Fellowship in this jurisdiction during the past forty years. No man was better or more favorably known, no one ever rendered more substantial and valuable benefits; no one ever gave more time, energies, and talents to advance the great interests of this Order, and no one ever endeared himself to the hearts of the whole brotherhood than he.

His unexpected death was a severe blow to our whole Order, and in this jurisdiction left as it were "an empty chair in each of our homes," and deep grief in every heart; but having reached the bounds beyond which he could not pass, God took him from us to Himself, and in the language of his favorite poem, which he so often repeated in the last year of his life, of him be it said—

> "The truer life drew nigher,
> The morning star climbed higher,
> Earth's hold on him grew slighter,
> The heavy burdens lighter,
> And the dawn immortal brighter,
>
> Every year."

To his bereaved widow, his orphan children, his relatives and intimate friends, the tenderest sympathies of this entire fraternity are hereby most kindly and respectfully tendered in a loss which to them can be but little short of irreparable.

Which was adopted by a rising vote.

Grand Representative A. H. Ransom, from the same committee, submitted the following report:

To the Grand Lodge of Kentucky:

Since the last annual communication of this Grand Body death has invaded its ranks and claimed as a victim one of its most prominent members, Past Grand Master William T. Curry, and we are thus again reminded that "in a few more years at most we shall be called to join those who have gone to their rest; our voice will be as silent, and our arm as powerless as theirs, and then all that will remain of us on earth will be the good or the evil that we have done."

Brother Curry was born in the city of Harrodsburg, Kentucky, January 6, 1823, and died in the same city April 21, 1882, at the age of 59—full of years, rich in love and confidence of the entire community in which he lived and died, leaving behind him a name honored and respected by all, and in the confident hope of a blessed immortality.

He was initiated in Montgomery Lodge No. 18, at Harrodsburg, but six months after the lodge was instituted, when he was 22 years of age; was installed Noble Grand in July, 1847, and was ever a faithful and zealous member of the lodge, and to him the lodge is indebted for much of its prosperity and its influence in the community.

In July, 1856, he became a member of this Grand Body, and with the exception of one year he was present at every session from that time until the year 1880, when he was prevented from attending by the sickness which, after eighteen months of intense suffering, terminated his life. His constant attendance, his zeal for the welfare of the Order, his valuable labors in the work of the Grand Lodge, and his affable and courteous demeanor in his intercourse with his brethren soon gained for him the high position in this Grand Body which was held by him to the close of his life. In 1869 he was elected by the Grand Encampment a Representative to the Sovereign Grand Lodge, and was continued as such until 1876—eight consecutive years. He soon gained and held a high position among its members as is shown by his service of one year on the Committee on Petitions, two years on the Committee on Finance, and five years on the Committee on State of the Order.

The record of such a life is a valuable legacy to all who survive, and should stimulate us to follow so worthy an example that when our work on earth is ended and we are called upon to surrender our trust we, too, may be received with the welcome salutation, "Well done thou good and faithful servant, enter thou into the joys of thy Lord."

Which was adopted by a rising vote.

Past Grand Master Geo. W. Morris, from the same committee, submitted the following report:

To the Grand Lodge of Kentucky:

Past Grand Master H. C. Pindell, whose death occurred about six months ago, united with our Order at Lexington, Kentucky, in the year 1848, at which time he was a young lawyer; he was finely educated, a close student, and for years prior to his death had won distinction at the bar; he arose rapidly in the Order, reaching the chair of Grand Master in 1852, within four years of the date of his initiation, and for several years following was among the most valuable, influential, and popular members of the Grand Lodge. In the later years of his life he rendered valuable service in forming and putting into operation the Benefit Association, and during several years was its President.

He was an upright judge, a conscientious lawyer, a consistent Christian, an eminent citizen, a true Odd Fellow, whose death is deeply deplored by all who knew him.

Past Grand A. B. Dean, an honored member of Chosen Friends Lodge No 2, died on December 10, 1881, of yellow fever at Havana, Cuba, where he had gone in the pursuit of his business.

In the prime and vigor of manhood, full of energy, of bright hopes and earnest purpose, in a strange land, away from home, family, and friends, he was suddenly removed from the trials, disappointments, and struggles of this earth to the rewards of the life beyond the grave.

As a Christian he was active and enthusiastic, coming up to the full measure of the rule to "visit the widows and the fatherless in their affliction."

As an Odd Fellow he was thorough, constant, and true to its principles, and in his daily walk he exemplified the principles he professed.

As a business man he was prompt, energetic, enterprising; prosperity did not allure him from the strict path of rectitude, nor did misfortune lessen his endeavors to overcome them.

As a citizen he was ever ready to do all in his power to advance the best interests of the city in which he lived.

As a parent he was kind, considerate, affectionate, and our heartfelt sympathies are hereby tendered his bereaved widow and orphan children.

Which was adopted by a rising vote.

Representative C. W. Harris, of No. 32, from the same committee, submitted the following report:

To the Grand Lodge of Kentucky:

It is with sorrow that your committee are called upon to chronicle the death of our brother, Past District Deputy Grand Master N. B. Shaller, of North Star Lodge No. 76, which occurred at his home in Newport January 17, 1882. Brother Shaller was a man whose mind and heart had both been broadened by extensive travel and large acquaintance with the world; a man who in his day and generation held a high rank in his chosen profession (medicine), and who fulfilled every duty entrusted to his hands with a fidelity that was proverbial—a graduate of Harvard, class of 1829, a graduate of the Boston School of Medicine. He was besides possessed of a fund of general information seldom surpassed by his cotemporaries. As a husband, father, son, and friend he was a very model.

He was initiated into the Order in Noah's Dove Lodge No. 20, May 4, 1846, and in 1850 he became one of the charter members of North Star Lodge, with which he remained in active membership to the time of his death.

The snows of more than threescore and ten winters had whitened his head, and, thank God, his heart was well. *Requiescat in pace.*

Which was adopted by a rising vote.

Past Grand Sire M. J. Durham, from the same committee, submitted the following reports:

To the Grand Lodge of Kentucky:

Past Chief Patriarch Francis Grief was born in San Wendel, Sax Coburg, Germany, September 29, 1808; emigrated to America with his father's family in 1834; settled in Paducah, Ky., in the year 1842; was initiated in Mangum Lodge No. 21, on January 7, 1847. He became a member of Mount Nebo Encampment No. 19, December 10, 1858. He was an Odd Fellow nearly thirty-six years, and never failed to attend a meeting of his lodge unless prevented by sickness. He died August 12, 1882. He was a good man, a zealous and consistent Odd Fellow, and a good citizen. His memory and his virtues will be templed in our hearts.

To the Grand Lodge of Kentucky:

Past Grand and Past Chief Patriarch Thomas Perry Holland was born in Fluvanna county, Virginia, October 6, 1822. His parents removed to Christian county, Kentucky, in 1834, and from thence to Trigg county, Kentucky, in 1836. He was married July 3, 1844, and located in McCracken county in 1849. Was initiated in Mangum Lodge No. 21 in 1853,, became a charter member and was the first Noble Grand of Lovelaceville Lodge in the latter part of the same year; was a charter member and first Noble Grand of Massac Lodge No. 137. He has several times represented his lodge in the Grand Lodge, and was noted for his zeal and devotion to Odd Fellowship.

On Tuesday, October 24, the day of the assembling of this Grand Lodge, he died. His funeral was on the following day, his remains being borne to burial within a few feet of his lodge-room, in accordance with his request, by his brother Odd Fellows.

Our brother was struck down by scarce a note of warning. The announcement of his death fell upon the heart of a grieved community, a large and widely distributed circle of friends, and a loving brotherhood like the sudden, deep tolling of a funeral bell upon a festival group. We have reason to believe that the remorseless stroke fell upon one well-prepared to receive it. His business probity, his stainless, private character, his personal virtues, all lead us to confidently say that there was a torchlight of comforting hope to illume the otherwise dark valley of the shadow of death.

He loved his family, his home, and his friends, and was ever grateful to God for the blessings he enjoyed.

We have nothing left us now but the memory of an unreproached name that is with Odd Fellows "as ointment poured forth."

To the Grand Lodge of Kentucky:

WHEREAS, it has pleased Divine Providence to remove from us by death our well-beloved brother, James L. Ridgely, therefore,

Resolved, That we recognize in this sad event, not only a great bereavement, but the loss of one who has done more to unite the human race in the ties of a common brotherhood than any man of his time.

Resolved, That while we can scarcely sorrow for the death of one who attained a ripe old age, whose work had been so well and so thoroughly done, and who leaves to his family and friends the fragrance of the memory of a well-spent and illustrious life, yet we find that this Order has sustained an irreparable loss, the loss of one who has conferred upon mankind benefits beyond the achievements of the warrior, the scholar, or philosopher.

Resolved, That as we survey the long and splendid career of our brother who has fallen at his post of duty, and to whose finished life the seal of death has now been set amid the universal regrets of his brethren, we shall best prove our love and veneration for his memory, not by indulging in fruitless repinings, but by borrowing inspiration and incentive from the sublime examples left us in the purity of his life and in the beneficience of the works which still follow him though he has rested from his labors.

Resolved, That cherishing for his memory a profound admiration and affection, we proffer to his bereaved family our sincerest sympathy and condolence.

Resolved, That the Secretary of this Grand Lodge transmit a copy of these resolutions to the family of James L. Ridgely.

Which were adopted by a rising vote.

www.ingramcontent.com/pod-product-compliance
Lightning Source LLC
Chambersburg PA
CBHW030902260626
47169CB00008B/2652